D1064349

The Cycling Wangdoos

by Kelly Pulley

1st Edition
Text & Illustrations © 2010 Kelly Pulley

Gauthier Publications
P.O. Box 806241
Saint Clair Shores, MI 48080
Attention: Permissions Department

Frog Legs Ink is an imprint of Gauthier Publications
www.FrogLegsInk.com

Proudly printed and bound in the USA
BP, Brainerd MN
May, 2011

ISBN: 978-0-9820812-1-1

Library of Congress Control Number: 2011929492

For my family, who shower me with endless love
and support.

For the Harpeth Bike Club, and all the members who
suggested I write a book about cycling.

For Vickie, the most optimistic, encouraging and
selfless person I know.

On the steep roads that wind round the peaks of Tibet,
Where the mountains reach higher than most mountains get.
The Cycling Wangdoos trained to bicycle race
Round the dangerous curves, at a perilous pace!

They worked as a team, knowing teamwork works best,
And they each did their part to support all the rest.
They found working as one made the work much more fun,
So instead of six bikes the Wangdoos rode on one.

The rider up front was the biggest Wangdoo,
His job was to steer and to pedal some too.
From the front to the back they sat biggest to small
So the furthest one back was the smallest of all.
Perched behind the Wangdoos on a rickety rack
Where his job was to sit, sat the team's mascot yak.

They rode up! They rode down!
They rode here! They rode there!

The people they passed on the road would just stare
As the Cycling Wangdoos rode to China and back
On their six seated bike with a yak on a rack.

They won races in Belgium and Italy too.
They rode races in Spain and won more than a few.

With them working as one, no one else stood a chance.
Until...

Leading a race up a mountain in France
The Wangdoo in the back sort-of fell in a trance.
And he started to thinking the thoughts that one thinks
When one thinks that the thing that they're thinking of stinks.

He thought to himself, "I'm the smallest Wangdoo,
All the other Wangdoos weigh much more than I do.
It just isn't fair for me here in the back
To do quite so much work hauling them and a yak!
And besides, they're so strong and I'm so very small
If I rested my legs, they won't notice at all."

Well, they hadn't gone far when the next Wangdoo saw
The Wangdoo in the back wasn't helping at all.
He said, "We're in a race, what's the matter with you?"
So the resting Wangdoo explained why he was through.
"It just isn't fair for me here in the back
To do quite so much work hauling them and a yak!
And besides, they're so strong and I'm so very small
If I rested my legs, they won't notice at all."

Now Wangdoo number five started thinking the same,
That the bigger Wandoos out in front were to blame
For the work that the smaller Wangdoos in the back
Had to do hauling bigger Wangdoos and a yak!
So he did just the same as the smaller Wangdoo
And said, "My days of helping the others are through!"

Well, they hadn't gone far when the next Wangdoo saw
The Wangdoos in the back were not helping at all.
She said, "We're in a race, what's the matter with you?"
So the resting Wangdoos explained why they were through.
"It just isn't fair for us here in the back
To do quite so much work hauling them and a yak!
And besides, they're so strong and we're so very small
If we rested our legs, they won't notice at all."

Soon the biggest Wangdoo did the work for them all
And their speed had slowed down to the pace of a crawl.
As he struggled alone just to make the bike go
Their fantastical speed was now slower than slow.

All the other teams' riders were all riding past
The Wangdoos went from riding in front place to last.

And then, as they crept to the top of the peak
Out of breath, the Wangdoo in the front turned to speak.
Though his vision was blurred from the sweat in his eyes
What he saw in the back gave him quite a surprise!
All the other Wangdoos were relaxed and reclined.
They all sat on their rears
And fell further behind.

He gasped, "We're in a race, what's the matter with you?"
So the resting Wangdoos explained why they were through.
When they finished, he said, "Well then, I'm finished too!"

So, nobody bothered to pedal or steer,
Just the yak on the rack did his job in the rear.
As the bike rolled down hill it was picking up speed.
They began moving up from the rear to the lead.

But with nobody steering, they soon missed a turn.
For the cycling Wangdoos it was now time to learn
That teamwork works best when you all work as one!
When someone's not in, you're all in-for-no-fun!

Now their six-seated bike with the yak on a rack
Was out of control! It was on the wrong track!
It bounced down the mountain past boulders and trees,
The Wangdoos jumping off, bumping heads, bruising knees!
Still the yak on the rack did his job in the rear.
Though the team was afraid, still the yak showed no fear.

With the team on the ground the bike bounced out of view.
The Wangdoos' chance of winning the race was now through.

They stood to their feet and began walking back.
They felt bad for themselves. No one thought of the yak.

When at last they arrived, the bike race was long done.
It was time to announce the bike rider who won.
The Wangdoos all felt hurt from the bruises they had,
Their bruised knees, their bruised pride, they all hurt really bad.
But the thing they now saw was the thing that hurt worst...

The Wangdoos finished last . . . but the yak finished first!